JOE WICKS

THE BURPEE BEARS

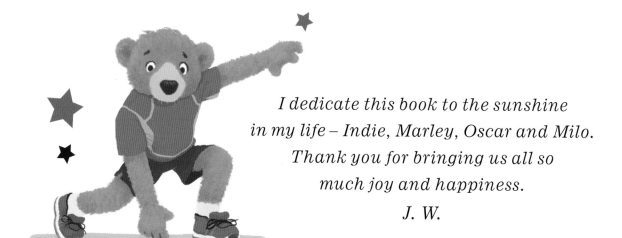

I dedicate this book to the sunshine
in my life – Indie, Marley, Oscar and Milo.
Thank you for bringing us all so
much joy and happiness.
J. W.

First published in hardback in Great Britain by HarperCollins *Children's Books* in 2021
HarperCollins *Children's Books* is a division of HarperCollins*Publishers* Ltd
1 London Bridge Street, London SE1 9GF

www.harpercollins.co.uk

HarperCollins*Publishers*
1st Floor, Watermarque Building, Ringsend Road, Dublin 4, Ireland

1 3 5 7 9 10 8 6 4 2

The Burpee Bears concept copyright © Joe Wicks 2021
Text copyright © Joe Wicks 2021
Illustrations copyright © Paul Howard 2021

ISBN: 978-0-00-850100-6

Joe Wicks and Paul Howard assert the moral right to be identified
as the author and illustrator of the work respectively.

A CIP catalogue record for this book is available from the British Library.

Printed in Italy

The tried-and-tested recipes in this book have been reviewed by a leading child nutritionist and carefully selected to suit most adults and children, but neither the publisher nor contributors can be held responsible for any adverse reaction to any of the ingredients. When using kitchen appliances you must always follow the manufacturer's instructions. Always allow hot liquids to cool before handling or blending. All exercises should be undertaken with adult supervision and due care. The exercises in this book have been carefully selected to benefit most adults and children, but neither the publisher nor contributors can be held responsible for any injuries related to these or similar physical activities.

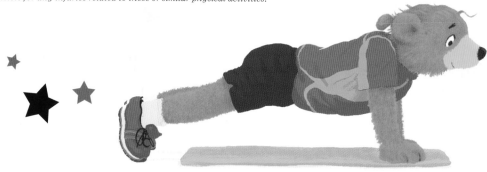

JOE WICKS

THE BURPEE BEARS

Story co-written with **Vivian French**
Illustrated by **Paul Howard**

HarperCollins *Children's Books*

The sun is rising
and the **Burpee Bears** are fast asleep.

Or
are
they?

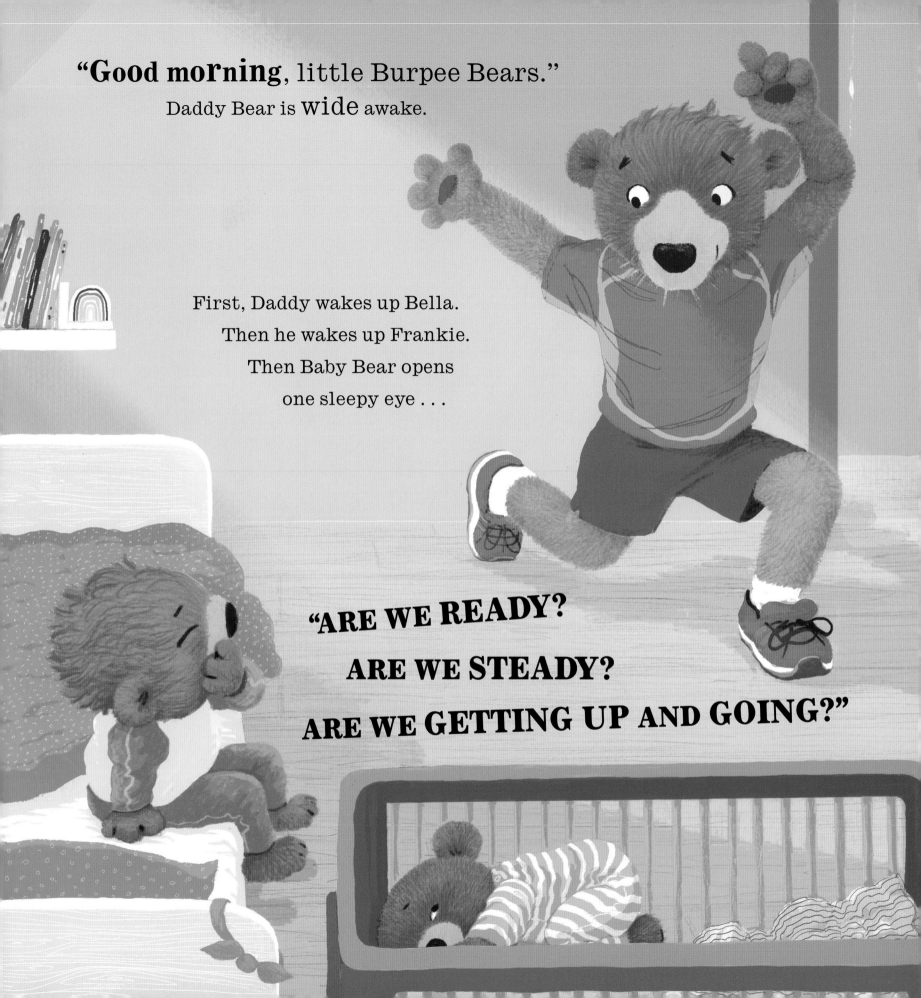

"**Good morning**, little Burpee Bears."
Daddy Bear is wide awake.

First, Daddy wakes up Bella.
Then he wakes up Frankie.
Then Baby Bear opens
one sleepy eye . . .

"ARE WE READY?
ARE WE STEADY?
ARE WE GETTING UP AND GOING?"

"Is it time to wake up Mummy?" asks Bella as she **stretches up,**

and **stretches down,**

and then **whirls round** and **round.**

Mummy Bear is snuggled up and snoozing under the duvet when . . .

One! **TWO!** **Three** little Burpee Bears jump on the bed.

"ARE WE READY?"

"ARE WE STEADY?"

"LET'S GET CUDDLING!"

Then Daddy Bear sets off to the kitchen to make breakfast.

"**Hooray,** it's a new day!" Bella says as she stops Baby Bear falling off the bed.
"Ray! Ray!" echoes Baby Bear.

"I'm an **astronaut,**" Frankie says. He zooms round and round the room, but then . . .

cRaSH!

"I'm SO hungry," wails Frankie.
"I'm too hungry to be an astronaut."

"Breakfast time!"
calls Daddy.

"Yippee," says Bella.
"It's sunshine juice
and porridge for breakfast!"

Frankie is still grumpy.
"I don't want porridge. I want banana
pancakes with honey."

"Why don't you try honey on your porridge?"
suggests Mummy.

Frankie tries a spoonful.

"YUMMY!
This porridge is **delicious!"**

"Hey," says Daddy Bear. "What are we going to do today, guys?"

Bella wants to watch TV.
Frankie plans to make a supersonic rocket ship.
Mummy has her toolbox at the ready.
"I'm all set to build the playhouse," she says.

"Come on, guys," says Daddy Bear.
"It's a sunny day. All those things can wait.

Let's GO OUTSIDE and have
a BIG family adventure."

"Hooray!" says Bella.
"Ray! Ray!" echoes Baby Bear.

But Frankie rubs his
nose, thinking about
his rocket ship.

Mummy Bear gives him a hug. "Did you know astronauts **love** going for walks outside? The fresh air gives them amazing ideas!"

"That's right." Daddy Bear picks up Baby Bear and twirls him round. "A walk in the woods clears their brains so they can work on **bigger** and **better** rockets."

"ARE WE READY?
ARE WE STEADY?
LET'S GET GOING!"

But **are** the Burpee Bears ready?

**"Where's my
water bottle?"**

calls Bella.

**"Help me find my
trainers,"**

says Frankie.

"POo-WEEEe!
What's that smell?"
asks Bella.

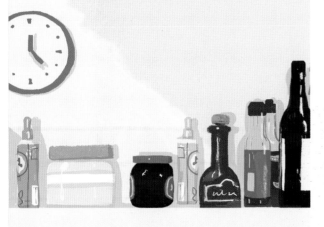

"**Oh no!**" says Mummy.
"Is it really lunchtime
already?"

"**Hooray!**"
says Frankie.
"I found my
trainers."

"**Great,**" says Daddy.
"So . . .

**ARE WE READY?
ARE WE STEADY?
CAN WE FINALLY
GET GOING?**"

"**YES, WE CAN!**"

they all say.
At last, the
Burpee Bears set
off for an adventure
in the woods.

Bella and Frankie chase each other through the leaves.

"'Eady, steady!" cheers Baby Bear.

But then . . .

"I'm tired," says Bella.

"Are we nearly there yet?" asks Frankie.

"Come on, superheroes!" says Daddy Bear.
"Let's pick up those tired toes!
Ready, steady – **lunge!**

And what about some bear crawls?
That's what bears do best."

Bella and Frankie lunge . . .

left leg . . .

right leg . . .

and do big bear crawls.

Then Bella says, "Let's try **frog jumps!**"

"ARE WE READY?"

"ARE WE STEADY?"

"LET'S GET JUMPING!"

And the Burpee Bears jump
their way to the top of the hill.

"BIG JUMP FOR THE WIN!"

they shout.

Bella and Frankie collect some sticks.
"Time to build my **rocket ship**," says Frankie.

Baby Bear and Daddy Bear find some
fiery red leaves.

Mummy Bear shows them what to do . . .

"ARE WE READY?"

"ARE WE STEADY?"

"LET'S GET BUILDING!"

But just as they finish . . .

... the rain starts to fall.

DRIP

DROP

DRIP

DROP

DRIP

DROP!

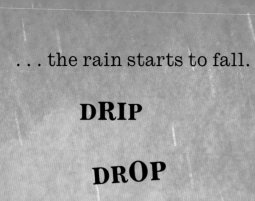

"Drip-drops?" says Baby Bear.

The rain falls **harder**.
The wind blows **stronger**.

SPLOSH
SPLASH
SPLOSH
SPLASH!

Bella dances
with **high**
knees through
the puddles.

Whoosh goes the wind.
Swish falls the rain.

WHOOSH
SWISH
WHOOSH!

"I'm scared,"
wails Frankie.

Oh no!
What are the
Burpee Bears
going to do?

"ARE WE READY?"

"ARE WE STEADY?"

"LET'S GET RUNNING!"

They run out of the rain and race into Frankie's rocket.

"We made it!" says Daddy Bear. "Well done, everybody."

"No drip-drops," says Baby Bear.

"Let's fly to the moon!" says Frankie.

"And touch the stars," says Bella.

"Let's have dinner first," says Mummy Bear.

"I think the rain will stop soon."

"ARE WE READY?
ARE WE STEADY?
LET'S GET COOKING!"

Together, they all get busy.
They make **veggie burgers**

and **fruit salad** for pudding.

They eat their dinner under the stars.

"Hey," says Mummy Bear, "have we had a fun day?"

"SO much fun," says Bella.

"Supersonic fun," says Frankie.

"Fun, fun," echoes Baby Bear.

"What did you love the most?" asks Daddy Bear.

"Seeing all those stars," says Bella.

"Building my rocket ship," says Frankie.

"'Eady, steady," whispers Baby Bear.

"I love **all of this**," says Mummy Bear. **"And all of you."**

"Time to go home, sleepyheads," says Daddy Bear.

"ARE WE READY?"

"ARE WE STEADY?"

"ARE WE FAST ASLEEP
AND DREAMING?"

Goodnight,
Burpee Bears.

WAKE-UP ROUTINE!

Are you ready? Are you steady? Then let's get going!

It doesn't matter how many exercises you do – just have fun! Why not start with five goes per exercise and build up?

1 JUMPING JACKS

Jump like a star with your arms and legs wide, then jump in . . . and repeat!

2 MOUNTAIN CLIMBERS

Get into a plank position with your back straight and tummy pulled in. Bring one knee in, then the other. Go as slow or fast as you like!

BURPEES

Stand with your feet shoulder-width apart and your arms by your sides.

Lower into a squat position and place your hands on the floor.

Kick or step your legs back into a plank position.

Jump or step your legs forward to return to a squat position.

Return to a standing position and jump in the air!

4

HIGH KNEES

Run on the spot and drive your knees up as high as you can. Go as slow or fast as you like!

5

BIG JUMP FOR THE WIN!

Squat down and touch the ground, then jump in the air . . . and repeat!

WIND-DOWN ROUTINE!

Are you ready for a gentle end to a busy day? You can do the whole routine all the way through as many times as you like. It may help you feel sleepy and relaxed. Try to keep breathing slowly and deeply as you go through the steps.

1 DOWNWARD DOG

Bend your knees and walk your hands out until your back is straight. Keep your knees a little bent if you need to!

2 REACH UP TO THE SUN

Put your right leg forward and reach your hands high in the air, with your arms by your ears. Then swap legs . . . and repeat!

3 TOUCH YOUR TOES

Bend from your hips and keep your back as straight as you can – don't worry if you don't reach your toes, just go as far as you are able without rounding your back too much.

4

SIT DOWN AND TOUCH YOUR TOES

Sit with your legs outstretched and your back straight. Bend from your hips and keep your back as straight as you can – don't worry if you don't reach your toes, just go as far as you are able without rounding your back too much.

5

TURN TO THE LEFT, TURN TO THE RIGHT

Gently cross your right leg over your left leg. Take a big breath in, then turn to the left as you breathe out. Then swap your legs over and repeat on the right side.

6

LIE DOWN FLAT AND THINK HAPPY THOUGHTS

This is the most important exercise of them all. Lie on your back, with your legs open hip-width and your arms by your sides. Let your thoughts come and go as you breathe deeply and feel your mind and body become still. Try to do this for two minutes.

FAMILY RECIPES WITH THE BURPEE BEARS

These recipes should each feed four bears!

Safety in the Kitchen

*Before starting work, wash everyone's hands thoroughly. Children **must always have** a grown-up to help them in the kitchen, and should never use sharp knives, a food processor or handle anything hot. Never leave a pan on the heat unattended and always take care when putting things in or taking things out of the oven.*

BANANA PANCAKES

INGREDIENTS

2 bananas, roughly chopped

2 eggs

50g rolled oats

2 tbsp yogurt

a little coconut oil, for greasing

METHOD

1. Whizz up the bananas, eggs and oats in a blender to make your batter.

2. Put a small amount of coconut oil in a non-stick frying pan over a medium heat.

3. Pour little puddles of batter into the pan (about three puddles each time is best) and cook for about 1 minute on each side.

TIP Sprinkle with berries and a spoonful of yogurt for added deliciousness

BANANA AND HONEY PORRIDGE

INGREDIENTS

250ml oat milk (or any kind of milk to suit you and your family)

1 ripe banana, roughly chopped

75g rolled oats

honey (to taste)

METHOD

1. Place the milk and banana in a blender, and blitz until smooth.

2. Pour the mixture over the oats and stir well.

3. Leave to soak in a sealable container in the fridge overnight.

4. When it's breakfast time, warm through gently in a pan, stirring as you go to stop it sticking. Then drizzle with honey and enjoy!

TIP Prepare the mixture the night before

TIP Mash bigger berries for little children

VEGGIE BURGERS

INGREDIENTS

175g carrots

175g cabbage

175g cauliflower

40g corn

60g green peas

400g tin of chickpeas, drained and rinsed

drizzle of olive oil

handful of chopped fresh herbs, such as parsley, dill or coriander

2 tbsp plain flour

burger buns

sliced tomato

lettuce leaves

TIP
Lovely with mayonnaise or ketchup too!

METHOD

1. Roughly chop the vegetables. Add the chickpeas and whizz them together in a food processor to make a rough paste.

2. In a non-stick pan, fry the paste well for 8–10 minutes. Mix in the herbs and switch off the heat. Allow the vegetable mixture to cool down to room temperature.

3. Divide the mixture into four and shape into round patties. They don't have to be perfect! Then roll them in flour on a floured surface or plate to hold them together.

4. Place the patties on a plate lined with baking paper and put in the fridge for about 30 minutes, or longer.

5. In the pan, heat the oil on a medium heat and add the patties. Turn down to a gentle heat and fry well for 3–4 minutes on each side.

6. Switch off the heat and allow to cool a little before serving between buns, with tomato slices and lettuce leaves, if you like!

FRUIT SALAD

INGREDIENTS

30g apples

30g melon

30g kiwi fruit

orange juice

METHOD

1. Peel the apples, cut into quarters and then take out the cores. Chop up into thin slices.

2. Cut the melon into quarters and remove the skin and seeds. Then cut into thin slices.

3. Peel and chop the kiwi fruit into thin slices.

4. Mix it all up in a bowl and add a splash of orange juice (to your taste).

You can choose a variety of fruit to mix up into a fruit salad. Why not try mashed berries and thin slices of pear, orange, grapefruit, banana or peach as well?

TIP
Delicious with yogurt or ice cream!

A Note from Joe

I really hope that you have all enjoyed my first adventure with the Burpee Bears. They are a busy family, but they know just how much fun it can be to spend time out and about, cooking and eating together. These are some of my favourite things in the world to do with my family.

I hope you'll feel inspired by my story to go on your own Burpee Bear adventures. Sometimes at bedtime we even talk about our favourite moments of the day, just like the Burpee Bears. I love to share the wonder of stories and books with my children.

Do have fun joining in the exercises at the end. Keep moving! Just a few small changes will make a difference. Let's make every day a healthy and happy one!

And I'd like to say a massive thank you to Vivian and Paul for helping bring my vision of the Burpee Bears to life. I just love everything about this book and the illustrations are fantastic. And thank you to Ann-Janine and everyone at HarperCollins for believing in my idea for the bears and giving me this wonderful opportunity to create my first picture book. And finally, thank you to all of you for reading my book.

I hope you keep going with the Burpee Bears . . . There are more adventures to come!

Lots of love,

Joe